...If we all had a wish in the Zoo!
I could change any part,
but where would I start?

And what would the animals do?

I don't want these stripes! roared the Tiger.
I wish I were more like you!

I'd be covered in spots
and some circles and dots!

Now, who was he talking to?

LEOPARD

I don't like this fur! growled the Brown Bear.
I want pink feathers like you!
I'd lay a big egg and then
stand on one leg!

Now,
who was she
talking to?

I want a long neck!
said the Hippo.
**I wish I were more like you!
I'd eat all the leaves
from the tops of the trees!**

Now, who was he talking to?

FLAMINGO

I don't want these paws!
cried the Panda.

I wish I were more like you!

I'd catch all the kippers with both of my flippers!

Now, who was he talking to?

I don't want this horn! said the Rhino.
I'd want a big shell like you!
If I needed to hide,
I could creep back inside!

Now, who was
she talking to?

I don't want green skin! said the Lizard.
I wish I were more like you!
I'd have a big hump
and a hairy brown rump!

**Now, who was
he talking to?**

I'd love two big ears!
hissed the Python.
I wissssssssh I were
more like you.
With an ear to the ground,
I'd hear every sound!

**Now, who was
she talking to?**

CAMEL

I don't want this hat!
said the Keeper.
I'd like a great mane
like you!
They'd all stop and stare
when they looked at
my hair!

Now, who was
she talking to?

LION

Now imagine this!

smiled the Keeper.

That all of these wishes came true.
So please take a look,
lift the flap in this book...

At a very
peculiar
ZOO!

For **Sally**

S.C.

For **Abby**
with love

L.E.H.

CLEANING IN PROGRESS

First published in 2007
by Meadowside Children's Books
185 Fleet Street
London EC4A 2HS
www.meadowsidebooks.com

A CIP catalogue record for this book
is available from the British Library
10 9 8 7 6 5 4 3 2 1
Printed in China